DENNIS the MENACE

A MENACE STRIKES BACK!

BEANObooks

published under licence by

meadowside 🍃
CHILDREN'S BOOKS

DENNIS THE DIRECTOR

"I'm really bored," said Dennis at breakfast.

Mum and Dad exchanged worried looks. When Dennis said he was bored, it usually meant trouble. Dad fished into his pocket and pulled out a five-pound note.

"Here you are, Dennis. Why don't you treat yourself to a film at the cinema," he said.

Dennis pushed the money into his pocket and gave a wide grin.

"Thanks, Dad!" He crammed the last piece of toast into his mouth and raced out of the door.

"He can't get up to any menacing

while he's watching a film," Dad told Mum.

At his front gate, Dennis bumped into his friends, Curly and Pie Face.

"Come on," he grinned, waving the five-pound note at them. "We're going to the cinema! What film do you wanna see?"

"A scary one!" said Curly and Pie Face at the same time.

They raced to Silver's Super Cinema and joined the queue for tickets. The cinema manager was serving at the ticket counter. His bushy black eyebrows were glowering and there was a scowl on his face. It got even worse when he saw Dennis, Curly and Pie Face.

"Not you lot again," he grumbled. "First my assistant goes off sick so I have to do some work and now you menaces turn up.

"Well, I'm warning you, any trouble and you're out!"

He jerked a thumb over his shoulder. Dennis, Curly and Pie Face just grinned at him and walked into the dark cinema. They went upstairs and sat in the little balcony area, right at the front.

"These are the best seats in the house but everyone always forgets about them," Dennis chuckled. "We'll have the balcony to ourselves!"

They settled down to watch the film. But soon the three menaces began to scowl. The film wasn't scary at all!

"What a rotten trick," whispered Curly. "All these people came here for a good scare, and this film wouldn't even scare a softy!"

"Maybe we should give them their money's worth!" suggested Dennis. "Quick – what have you got in your pockets?"

Curly and Pie Face emptied their pockets at top speed. Between them they had five earwigs, eight spiders, four catapults (Dennis always carried a spare for emergencies), two bird whistles, three feathers and a ball of string. A smile spread over Dennis's face. It was a smile Curly and Pie Face knew very well. It meant that a menace was on the way!

Dennis picked up the feathers and tied a long piece of string to the end of each one. Then they dangled the feathers over the edge of the balcony.

"Arghh!"
"Eeek!"

The people in the row below screamed as they felt the feathers brush the backs of their necks.

Dennis, Curly and Pie Face whipped the feathers out of sight.

"Shhh!" hissed the cinema manager, who couldn't see the feathers in the dark. He thought they were screaming at the film and he didn't like to hear anyone having too much fun.

Next Dennis picked up a bird whistle. He cupped it in his hands and began to make a faint, ghostly, hooting sound. The people in the audience started to turn around, trying to work out where the spooky noise was coming from. Pie Face and Curly stuffed their fists into their mouths to stop giggling. People were holding on to each other and shivering in fear.

"It's ghosts!" quivered one lady.

"A haunted cinema!" trembled her friend.

"This cinema is not haunted!" seethed the manager. But no one was listening to him.

Next Dennis, Pie Face and Curly picked up their catapults together with the earwigs and spiders they had been keeping. TWANG! Dennis sent a spider somersaulting through the air. ZING! An earwig shot from Curly's catapult.

"Arghh!" screamed a man as an earwig landed in his popcorn.

"Help!" squeaked a woman as two spiders dangled from her earrings.

Within seconds everyone was on their feet, jumping around and screaming. On screen the actress had just walked into a haunted house, but the film was completely forgotten. The audience rushed out, fighting to be first through the door. The manager narrowed his eyes. His bushy eyebrows waggled angrily and he looked up at the balcony.

"Oh, ghosts and insects is it?" he muttered furiously. "That really is the last straw!"

He ran up to the balcony three steps at a time and grabbed Curly and Pie Face by the collars, yelling as he dragged them downstairs.

"You menaces are banned once and for all!" he bellowed as he dragged them through the angry crowd of people, who were all demanding their money back.

"You shouldn't show such boring films, then!" Dennis roared as he followed Pie Face and Curly out to the street. They had been dropped in a muddy puddle. The manager slammed the door behind them and

Dennis stomped off down the street.

"We've gotta teach that old bully a lesson!" he stormed. Then he skidded to a halt. A crowd of softies was gathered on the pavement ahead. Walter was there with Spotty Perkins and Bertie Blenkinsop.

"What's going on here?" Dennis asked. Walter turned around.

"Oh it's you riff-raff!" he said rudely. "This is not for menaces like you, Dennis."

"Oh yeah?" growled Dennis. Softies went flying right and left as he elbowed his the way through the crowd. He saw a large poster on the wall.

HOLLYWOOD COMES TO BEANOTOWN

A CHANCE TO BE A DIRECTOR

MAKE YOUR OWN FILM AND WIN A FANTASTIC PRIZE!

"Excellent!" grinned Dennis. "If we can't watch films any more, we can make 'em!"

"Haw haw," sneered Walter. "As if a menace like you knows anything about directing! I'm going to make a film about scented flowers and twittering birds and pretty trees. If I'm very lucky, I might even see a fairy at the bottom of my garden!"

"There's no such thing as fairies!" scoffed Dennis.

"What?" squeaked one of the softies in dismay.

"Don't listen to him," said Walter. "My film is going to be the best, and with Mumsy's super-duper new video camera I am bound to win!"

"With a film about flowers and fairies!" guffawed Dennis. "Fat chance!"

He turned to Pie Face and Curly. "There's no way a softy's gonna beat us!" he said, thumping his fist into his palm.

"Come on, menaces – were gonna be film directors!"

They raced back to Dennis's house and found Dad's old video camera in a box under the stairs. It was held together with elastic bands and sticky tape.

"It's falling to bits!" Curly complained.

"It's what you film that counts – not the camera!" grinned Dennis. "And Walter's flowers can't beat what we're about to film!"

"What's that?" asked Pie Face.

"Menacing!" Dennis said.

13

Dennis, Curly and Pie Face had a busy week.

On Monday they filmed his neighbour the Colonel. Dennis and Curly crept into his garden, where he was putting his soldier dolls through their paces.

"Hup two three four! Hup two three four! Keep marching!" the Colonel bellowed. Dennis grinned into the camera lens.

"This is the Colonel," he whispered into the microphone. "He's as nutty as a fruitcake!"

"I heard that!" roared the Colonel, grabbing Dennis by the scruff of the neck and giving him a shake.

"You little menace!"

"Gnasher, quick!" shouted Dennis. Gnasher leapt up and took a huge bite out of the seat of the Colonel's trousers. He shot into the air, clutching his bottom and letting go of Dennis.

"RUN!" Dennis yelled. "Keep filming, Curly!"

The Colonel chased Dennis through all the back gardens, leaping over fences as if they were hurdles in a race.

"Come back here! You'll be court-martialled!" the Colonel thundered. Dennis shot through a small gap in a fence, closely followed by Gnasher, Curly and Pie Face. The Colonel was so angry he didn't stop! He threw himself  into the gap and got stuck halfway through. On one side of the fence his legs kicked in the air, while on the other his nose was tickled by Dennis's mum's sunflowers!

"You stop that filming at once – **ACHOO!** – and get me out of here!" the Colonel stormed. But Dennis and his cameramen were disappearing into the distance!

On Tuesday they filmed Walter the Softy. He was out for a walk with his girlfriend Matilda and they passed Dennis's house. Dennis was just spraying Curly with the garden hose when he heard Walter's voice.

"These are for you, Matilda," he said. "I picked them myself!"

Dennis and Curly peered over the garden hedge. Walter had just handed Matilda a bunch of flowers, tied with a pink ribbon.

"Yuck!" said Curly, sticking out his tongue.

"You're so wonderful, Walter," said Matilda. " I'll put them in some water to keep them fresh and beautiful, just like me."

"Ugghh!" cried Dennis, "I've heard enough!" He switched on the hose and blasted the bunch of flowers with it. "That'll keep 'em wet – and you too!" he chortled. Walter and Matilda were soaked from head to foot!

"You scoundrel!" spluttered Matilda. "You've ruined my hairstyle and it took Mumsy hours this morning!"

"Well, all little flowers need watering!" guffawed Curly.

On Wednesday they filmed Sergeant Slipper. Roger the Dodger lent them one of his best dodges – a pound coin on the end of a fishing line. They put it on the pavement where Sergeant Slipper walked on his beat. When he saw the pound he bent down eagerly to grab it, but Dennis jerked the fishing rod and the pound leapt away from the policeman.

"Oy, come back here!" he bellowed, chasing the pound coin. But every time he bent to pick it up, it was whisked out of his reach.

Sergeant Slipper chased the pound

coin all the way through Beanotown. He splashed through muddy puddles and charged through crowds, sending people flying in all directions.

"Must... get... the money..." he puffed. His blue uniform was splattered with mud and his helmet was wonky, but he didn't care. All he wanted was to catch that pound!

With one final determined roar he leapt through the air at the coin... and sprawled at the feet of the Chief Inspector!

"**SLIPPER!**" roared the Chief Inspector. "What is the meaning of this?"

Dennis pulled the coin out of sight and raced off with Curly and Pie Face, chortling.

On Thursday they filmed Minnie the Minx. There was a party in her garden because her cousin was getting married and Minnie was wearing a pink frilly dress!

"Look at Minnie!" hooted Dennis, filming her over the fence.

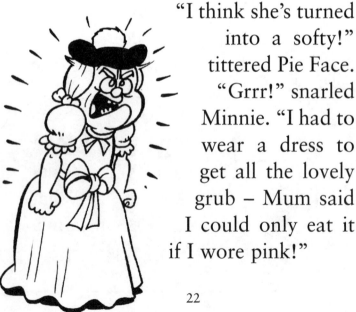

"I think she's turned into a softy!" tittered Pie Face.

"Grrr!" snarled Minnie. "I had to wear a dress to get all the lovely grub – Mum said I could only eat it if I wore pink!"

22

"A likely story!" chuckled Dennis. Minnie clenched her fists.

"I'll show you I'm not a softy!" she growled. She leapt over the fence to chase them – straight into next door's pile of manure!

"Pwoaar, what a pong!" cried Dennis, holding his nose.

"Frilly and stinky!" grinned Pie Face.

Just then Minnie's mum peered over the fence. When she saw Minnie she went purple in the face.

"I warned you!" she spluttered. "Up to your room, right now! There'll be no party food for you!"

On Friday they filmed Bea. She wanted to repaint her room and Dennis agreed to help her. They lined up pots of yellow, red and green paint.

"Ready, Bea?" asked Dennis.

"GO!" squealed Bea.

Dennis picked her up and dipped her hands and feet into the green paint. Then he held her up to the wall so that she could make her own patterns!

"More!" Bea shouted. They did the same with the red and yellow paint, until all the walls were covered with a bright new design. Bea clapped her paint-filled hands together. She crawled out of her room and downstairs. Dennis grabbed the camera and followed her.

"That's right, Bea!" he chortled, as she crawled around the sitting room. "Mum's always saying she wants the house redecorated!"

Soon every room in the house was covered with green, yellow and blue handprints and footprints.

"Nice!" cooed Bea.

"EEEK!" screamed Mum as she walked in and dropped all her shopping bags. "DENNIS!"

But Dennis and Bea had vanished!

At last it was time to watch the finished films. The whole of Beanotown crammed into the cinema. The judge was Mr Silver, the owner of the cinema.

While all the softies' films were playing, Mr Silver's eyes kept drooping. During Walter's film, he started to snore after the fortieth shot of a geranium. At last there was only one film left to watch. The title flashed up on the screen:

A MENACE STRIKES BACK!

The audience gasped as the film opened with a shot of the Colonel stuck halfway through the garden fence with his nose in a sunflower.

"There's only one good use for flowers when you're a menace," said Dennis's voiceover. Mr Silver roared with laughter. The Colonel said "Hurrumph!" very loudly from the back of the cinema.

They watched as the film unfolded. When Minnie landed in the manure, Mr Silver had to wipe tears of laughter from his eyes. As the film ended and the lights came up, he leaned over and shook Dennis by the hand.

"A hilarious film, young man! Takes me back to my youth!"

"And what about my little darling's film?" trumpeted Walter's Mumsy crossly.

Mr Silver cleared his throat and stood up to address the audience.

"There have been some, er, interesting entries," he said. "I think we have all learned a lot of things about geraniums that we never knew before."

"And never wanted to know!" added Dennis in a loud whisper. Mum threw him a warning look.

"But there is a clear winner," Mr Silver continued. "A hilarious comedy film, where the acting was so real I could almost believe that people were actually being menaced! Congratulations lads – the prize goes to Dennis, Curly and Pie Face!"

There was loud applause from their parents and angry mutterings from everyone else. The Colonel tried to say something but only let out a strange, gurgling sound.

"The prize is a wonderful one for budding film makers," continued Mr Silver. "Free tickets for a year into my cinema!"

"Awesome!" cheered Dennis.

"Mega!" shouted Pie Face and Curly.

"Oh no," groaned the manager, burying his head in his hands.

Dennis, Curly and Pie Face went up to Mr Silver to collect their prizes. He shook their hands and congratulated them again. "But there's one thing I want to know," he said. "How did you get all those people to pretend to be menaced in your film?"

"Oh, that was easy," chortled Dennis. "It just came naturally!"

GNASHER'S CARNIVAL CHAOS

"Oh, Gno," muttered Gnasher to himself. He was worried. He and Dennis were supposed to be going to the carnival with Curly and Pie Face, but Mum was holding onto his collar very tightly, and Gnasher had a horrible feeling that he knew why.

"Gnasher's staying here with me," she said.

"No way!"

bellowed Dennis.

"This Tripe Hound needs a bath – it is two years since his last one and he's starting to attract flies," said Mum firmly.

"But I like this smell!" Gnasher thought. It had taken him two years to build up the perfect odour and now Mum wanted to take it away from him!

Dennis raged and Gnasher struggled, but in the end Dennis had to go without him. Mum let go of Gnasher to pull on her thickest pair of rubber gloves. Then she turned to him and put her hands on her hips.

"Right," she said through gritted teeth. "I'm not looking forward to this any more than you are. But by the time I'm finished with you, you're going to smell like roses."

"Oh, yeah?" growled Gnasher. "Wanna bet?"

The great chase began! Gnasher weaved through chair legs and crawled under sofas. He balanced on the curtain rail and tried to climb up the chimney. He kicked cushions under Mum's feet and attempted to escape through the letterbox. But it was no use. Finally Mum clutched him in a grip of iron, marched into the bathroom and locked the door.

It was a very unpleasant half hour indeed.

At the end of it, Mum unlocked the bathroom door. She was covered in soot, soap, black hairs and water. Gnasher raced downstairs. He was dripping with water and smelled equally of roses and wet dog. Dad saw him coming and opened the front door to let him out. Gnasher pounded down the garden path with a wild look in his eyes.

"Phew!" said Dad as Mum crawled out of the bathroom on her hands and knees. "What's that horrible pong?"

"Tea and lots of it!" gibbered Mum. "I'm not doing that for another two years at least!"

Gnasher pelted down the street, filled with shame. The scent of roses followed him wherever he went! He splashed through muddy puddles and rolled in all the dirt he could find. But somehow the  strong smell of roses would  not leave. By the time he reached the centre of Beanotown, he was fuming. And that was when he spotted Foo-Foo.

Usually, Foo-Foo would have smelt Gnasher coming, but this time he didn't notice a thing. Gnasher crept up behind him on the tips of his toes. He waited until he was right behind him before letting out a loud

"GNASH!"

Perhaps this rosy smell had some benefits after all! Foo-Foo shot into the air like a rocket and landed in Walter's arms, quivering.

"Bad dog!" cried Walter. Gnasher bared his teeth and grabbed a mouthful of Walter's pink socks.

"Eeek!" Walter squealed, trying to run away. "Let me go, you horrid beast! I have to get to the dog show at the carnival!"

"Dog show! Gnash!" barked Gnasher. "That's for softy dogs!"

He chased after Walter and Foo-Foo. They ran to the field where the carnival was being held. Gnasher lost sight of them in the crowd, but he didn't care. There were more ankles to bite here than he had ever seen in one place!

Gnasher raced into the crowd with delight, getting ready to practise his best gnawing techniques. He spotted a pair of socks that really deserved gnashing – they were covered with

pictures of flowers and kittens, and they belonged to Walter's girlfriend Matilda.

38

But just as Gnasher opened his mouth ready to chomp, he saw something that stopped him in his tracks. He stayed as if he had been frozen, with one paw in the air and his mouth hanging open. The smell of roses stopped bothering him. He forgot all about the flowery socks. There, straight ahead of him, was a beautiful white tripe hound!

Gnasher was smitten! He bounded up to her.

"My name's Gnasher," he began, but she didn't let him finish. She bared her sharp white teeth and growled at him.

"I've got no time to talk to Tripe Hounds who smell of roses," she snapped. "I'm a carnival dog, and I've got a dog show to judge!"

"I don't usually smell like this," blushed Gnasher.

"I should hope not! Now clear off and stop bothering me!"

With a powerful back kick, the amazing creature sent Gnasher tumbling back into the crowd. Gnasher sat up and rubbed his head as he watched her leave.

"What a gorgeous kick!" he thought dreamily.

Not far away, Dennis, Pie Face and Curly were busy trying out some carnival games.

First they visited the coconut shy.

"I'll have the first shot," said

Dennis, getting his throwing arm ready. He hit the coconuts so hard that they split open and showered the man in charge with coconut milk. The three menaces guffawed loudly.

The first time it happened the man gave a tight smile and handed over Dennis's prize – a coconut.

The second time (Curly's turn) he didn't smile at all.

And when Pie Face did the same thing he scowled as he wiped coconut milk out of his eyes. Dennis stepped up for another turn. He took aim, fired and... **POW!**

"Clear off, you menaces!" the man roared, as his coconuts were smashed to pieces for the fourth time and he was drenched in coconut milk. "I'm running out of coconuts!"

41

Next they tried the helter skelter, but Dennis went so fast that he caught the other two up on the first bend! Curly and Pie Face flew off the helter skelter and landed on top of the woman who was running it.

"You're all b a n n e d ! " she shrieked as soon as Curly had clambered off her.

In the plate smashing game, Dennis was unhappy with the squashy balls they were given to throw.

"These softy balls don't smash anything!" he complained. His hand reached around to his back pocket. He pulled out his favourite catapult. He pulled out the coconut he had won. Pie Face and Curly chortled as Dennis loaded the coconut into his catapult, aimed at the plates and...

SMASH!

The coconut whizzed through the air, broke half the plates and shot a hole through the back of the stand, which gave a little wobble and folded up like a concertina!

"What a mega menace!" chortled Curly.

GRRRR! began the stand's owner.

"Run!" yelled Pie Face.

When they played hit the rat, Dennis hit it so hard that he broke the game in two. And finally the only thing they hadn't visited was the big top. Some clowns were fooling around by the entrance and there was a big sign over the door that read:

"Ha," scoffed Dennis as he saw Walter the Softy go in with Foo-Foo. "What a load of softy dogs! Who'd want a stupid rosette anyway?"

The others agreed and they started to leave, but Dennis found he couldn't move. When he looked down, he saw that Gnasher had his jumper in a tight grip and was pulling him towards the big top.

"You don't wanna go in there!" cried Dennis in alarm. "It's full of softies! And what's that smell of roses? What has Mum done to you, Gnasher?"

But Gnasher kept pulling.

"Good luck!" chortled Pie Face as Dennis disappeared inside the big top.

"Yeah, enjoy the show, mate!" guffawed Curly as they scarpered. Dennis wanted to go with them, but Gnasher had pulled him up to the registration table.

"Name?" asked the girl behind the table. She was scowling as much as Dennis was, and next to her was a white Tripe Hound. Dennis stared at it, and the girl stared at Gnasher.

"Nice dog!" they both said at the same time.

"This is Gnasher," said Dennis.

"This is Gnarla," said the girl. "She's gonna help me judge this stupid competition. I'd rather be running the coconut shy, but they forced us into it. I'm Dannie."

"Now I get it," said Dennis with a scowl. "GIRLS! Ok Gnasher, if you wanna impress Gnarla, you can enter the contest. Just don't go softy on me!"

Gnasher gave a menacing little growl.

The first event was a dog race. There were four dogs entered – Gnasher, Foo-Foo (covered in ribbons), Spotty Perkins's Pekinese, Sweetums, and Bertie Blenkinsop's sausage dog, Twinkle.

"Think you can beat them?" chuckled Dennis.

"Gnash!" barked Gnasher. He could see that Gnarla was watching and he was looking forward to showing off his speed and strength.

The dogs stood at one end of the track and the owners stood at the other, holding out their dog's favourite food. Walter held out a limp piece of lettuce. Spotty and

Bertie held out fairy cakes. Dennis held out a string of sausages. Dannie stood next to the dogs and held up her starter pistol. She looked even more furious than before.

"GO!" she yelled, firing the pistol. Foo-Foo skipped forward. Twinkle was so scared by the noise and the sight of the sausages that she ran straight up a passing gent's trouser leg. Sweetums hid his face behind his paws and sat yelping pitifully. Gnasher gave a loud bark and ran after Foo-Foo, leapfrogged over his back and reached the finish line first!

"The Tripe Hound wins the first contest!" announced Dannie.

"It's a fix!" sobbed Walter. "Cheat!"

"I saw no cheating, you softy," snapped Dannie. "Come on, I wanna get this over with. Next event – the agility trials!"

The agility course had been set up in another corner of the big top. There were jumps, tunnels to run through, hoops to leap through and seesaws to balance on. Dennis rubbed his hands together.

"This'll be easy for you, Gnasher, with all the escaping we've had to do!"

Gnarla was watching carefully. Gnasher puffed out his chest and took his place at the starting line. Dennis sat down and munched on one of Gnasher's sausages.

"You're supposed to run around the course with him, you know," simpered Walter. "Don't you know anything about showing dogs?"

"Gnasher doesn't need anyone to show him what to do," chortled Dennis. **"He's not a softy dog!"**

Dannie fired the starting pistol and Gnasher sailed over the first jump. He shot through the tunnel and balanced easily on the seesaw. He somersaulted through the air and tumbled through three hoops.

"Easy," thought Gnasher as he strolled back to the starting line. He hoped Gnarla was watching.

Foo-Foo was next, but he had got an attack of nerves. Walter was trying to encourage him.

"Don't be afraid, Foo-Foo darling," he whispered. "I know it's scary, but it will all be over soon!"

"What's scary about it?" scoffed Dennis. His grin widened as he had one of his brilliant ideas "I know, Gnasher will go round with him and show him how to do it!"

"No!" trembled Walter, but it was too late. Gnasher gave Foo-Foo a little nip on the tail to get him started and Foo-Foo sprang into the air and smashed into the first jump. The poles crashed to the ground and Foo-Foo landed on them in a heap.

"*YOWWL!*" cried Foo-Foo.

"Gnash! Get up!" Gnasher ordered. **"Keep going!"**

"Get on with it!" growled Dannie.

Foo-Foo ran towards the plastic tunnel but stopped suddenly at the entrance, quivering.

"*Poor Foo-Foo doesn't like tunnels!*" cried Walter, running after him. But before he could get there, Gnasher headbutted Foo-Foo's bottom. With a yelp Foo-Foo dived into the tunnel. Gnasher jumped on top of it and chased Foo-Foo out by squashing it. By this time Foo-Foo was panting, his ribbons were coming loose and his hair was getting frizzy.

"What are you doing to my poor Foo-Foo?" squeaked Walter. Foo-Foo tore around the course, sending jumps and tests flying in all directions.

"He's helping him finish the course!" guffawed Dennis as Foo-Foo tried to balance on the seesaw. Finally Gnasher jumped on the other end of it and the two dogs seesawed up and down so fast that Foo-Foo went green and the seesaw came off its base!

"He's finished the course all right," grinned Dannie,

looking at the wrecked agility trial. "It's fine by me! If it's broken, the other two can't finish it! Next – the obedience trials!"

Sweetums and Twinkle heaved sighs of relief.

"Foo-Foo will sail through this!" boasted Walter. "He's the most obedient dog in Beanotown!"

Dennis looked at the chaos Gnasher had created so far and grinned.

"I thought this was gonna be a softy trial," he chortled, "but it's ended up being the best menace of the week!"

For the obedience trials the dogs had to sit in front of a large bowl of their favourite food, but not touch it until their owners said so. While they waited they had to perform tricks.

"Pirouette on the spot, Foo-Foo!" called Walter. Foo-Foo stood up on his spindly back legs and did a little pirouette.

"Roly poly!" called Bertie. Twinkle tried to do a roly poly but just ended up tying herself into a tangled knot.

"Balance a ball on your nose!" called Bertie. But the ball was as bit as Sweetums and he was squashed under it!

"I don't reckon you can get a tripe

hound to balance a ball on his nose or do a pirouette!" chortled Dannie.

"The trick is," Dennis told Dannie, "to ask your Tripe Hound to do something he wants to do! Gnasher – menace 'em!"

Gnasher leapt into action! He nibbled Foo-Foo's kneecaps and gnashed Walter's ankles. He headed Sweetums's ball into Twinkle's stomach and unknotted her.

"Stop!" shrieked Walter. "This isn't how you run a dog show!"

Gnasher ran after the ball to show Gnarla his footballing skills. He kicked it to Dennis, who dribbled it past the wrecked agility course. Dennis weaved between Dannie and Gnarla and flicked the ball back to Gnasher, who gave it a powerful header... straight into the central support of the big top!

The support creaked.

It started to lean sideways.

The big top trembled... swayed... and...

CRASH!

The whole canopy collapsed around them!

There were shouts, screams and whimpers from the three softies and their dogs.

There were guffaws and barks from Dennis, Gnasher, Dannie and Gnarla.

They all clambered out of the end of the tent. The softies staggered away with their dogs as Dannie handed Dennis a huge red rosette.

"I declare you the winner of the Most Menacing Dog Show Ever!" she chortled.

Gnarla gave Gnasher a wink.
"Next stop Grrrufts!" she barked.
"See you at next year's carnival!"

MOUNTAINTOP MENACE

It was amazing. It was a miracle. Dad had entered a competition and actually WON it! He had come first in a spot-the-difference competition and the first prize was a family skiing holiday.

"The first time EVER!" whooped Dad, punching the air with his fist. "I'm a winner!"

"You're a right nutter," Dennis corrected. "You've never been skiing in your life! I can't wait to see this!"

Dad's eyes narrowed. "And what makes you think you'll be seeing anything?" he asked. "I haven't forgotten our last holiday, you pest.

"We don't want to get banned from anywhere else!"

Dennis folded his arms, lowered his eyebrows and stuck out his bottom lip.

"I want to come too!" he growled.

"Dad and I needed a holiday when we came back from the last one!" twittered Mum. "I want a nice relaxing break!"

"We'll get someone to come and look after you for the week," Dad went on.

"Perhaps the Colonel...?" Mum put in.

"Huh, I don't need anyone to look after me," Dennis argued. "Anyway, I wanna come! And you won't get anyone to look after me."

He was right. Troops of possible Dennis-sitters came, met Dennis and left at top speed. Not one of them lasted longer than ten minutes. Finally Mum and Dad were forced to take Dennis with them.

"But there must be no peashooters!" warned Dad.

"No whoopee cushions!" Mum added. **"AND NO MENACING!"** they said together. "Or you'll be on the first plane home!"

Dennis just grinned. He was looking forward to seeing Mum and Dad on skis.

"Skiing's for softies," he told Gnasher. "I'm gonna be a snowboarder!"

Mum, Dad, Bea and Dennis flew to the ski resort in a small plane. The captain of the plane had only ever met nice, well-behaved little boys. He didn't know about menaces. So he asked if Dennis would like to go into the cockpit and see all the controls. Mum and Dad tried to tell the captain it was a bad idea.

"You'll regret it," Mum said.

"And we want to arrive in one piece," added Dad.

But he just smiled and thought they were joking. So Dennis went into the cockpit. Mum and Dad crossed their fingers and hid behind their magazines.

The captain stayed calm when Dennis blew a very loud raspberry at air traffic control over the radio. Pilots are trained to deal with all sorts of emergencies.

He bit his lip very hard when Dennis pressed a big red button and oxygen masks dropped onto all the passengers' heads. But he still didn't lose his cool.

It was only when Dennis leaned against the controls and nearly crashed the plane into a mountain that the captain changed his mind. He pulled at the controls and the plane rose steeply, just missing the mountaintop.

"Get back to your seat!" he bellowed as soon as he had swerved around the mountain. Sweat was dripping down his forehead. "And don't move until we land!"

When the plane landed, Dennis was the first passenger off. Mum and Dad went to collect the luggage.

The captain was carried away on a stretcher, gibbering. In all his years of pilot training he had never been prepared for anything like Dennis.

"I tried to warn him," sighed Mum wearily.

The ski resort was covered in snow and the sun was shining. The sky was blue.

"How lovely," said Mum as they looked around their chalet. When they walked into the sitting room they met the family they would have to share it with. Dennis groaned. Standing in between his parents was the softiest softy he had ever seen (apart from Walter, of course).

"We're Mr and Mrs Finch-Salmon, and this is our son Cedric," said the man. Dad and Mr Finch-Salmon shook hands and started talking about the weather. Cedric walked up to Dennis with a horrible smirk on his face. His nose was stuck up in the air.

"I am an excellent skier," he drawled. "I have been skiing since I was a toddler. I can ski backwards. Have you ever been skiing?"

69

Dennis looked him up and down. Cedric was wearing a bow tie and his legs were slightly bandy. "Nah," Dennis shrugged. "But it can't be that difficult if you can do it. Anyway, I'm not going to be skiing, only snowboarding"

Cedric stuck his nose even higher in the air.

"Daddy says snowboarding is common," he said. "I suppose it will suit YOU."

"Oh yeah?" rumbled Dennis, clenching his fists. "Listen here, softy features…"

"DENNIS!" snapped Dad, clamping his hand down on Dennis's shoulder. "I want you to make friends with this nice young man."

"How do you do, sir," simpered Cedric. Dennis scowled at him.

Anyone who could suck up to parents like that could do anything! As soon as Dad walked away, Cedric leaned towards him with a smirk.

"Watching you trying to move along on the snow will be a good laugh. You'll spend most of the week upside down in snowdrifts! Haw haw!"

"Grrr, I'll wipe that smile off your face with my snowboard!" growled Dennis through gritted teeth. Cedric smirked again and then let out a false wail.

"Daddy! This nasty boy threatened me!"

"What?" snorted Mr Finch-Salmon.

"Dennis! **BED!**" roared Dad. Dennis stomped off to the bathroom with his hands in his pockets. Perhaps this holiday wasn't such a good thing after all!

When Dennis came out of the bathroom, Cedric was standing there with his towel. He screwed up his face in disgust when he saw Dennis.

"Ugh," sneered Cedric. "How dirty you are. Aren't you going to have an evening bath? I have one every morning and evening."

"Weirdo," muttered Dennis. Then he remembered something. His hand reached into his pocket and a menacing grin spread across his face.

Mum and Dad had said no peashooters and no whoopee cushions, but they hadn't mentioned anything else. Dennis ducked back inside the bathroom and quickly put the soap into his pocket. Then he replaced it with the trick soap he had borrowed from Curly.

"Bathroom's all yours," he told Cedric.

Dennis went to his room and waited. He heard the bath water running and he heard Cedric splashing. Then he heard the bath water drain away. Dennis sniggered and whispered to himself, "Five, four, three, two, one..."

"EEEEEK!" There was a piercing scream from the bathroom! "Mummy! Daddy!"

Dennis ran into the corridor just in time. Cedric was standing in the doorway of the bathroom in his pyjamas. He was yelling at the top of his reedy voice. He was completely blue and glowing!

73

"Good one, Curly!"

thought Dennis.

"This is your fault, you menace!" thundered Mr Finch-Salmon.

"What on earth have you done to my little Cedricy Wedricy?" cried Mrs Finch-Salmon.

Dennis just chortled, then dived back into his room as he saw Mum coming towards him. He didn't want to be sent home just yet!

Next morning, Dennis, Bea, Mum and Dad went to be fitted for skis and snowboards. Then they met their instructor. He took them to the stop of a little slope.

"This is called a nursery slope," he said cheerfully. "It's where you will learn to ski before you're allowed on the big slopes."

Just then, Dennis saw Cedric ski past at top speed. (He still had a faint blue tinge.)

"You'll be on the nursery slope all week!" Cedric called out as he went by.

"Oh yeah?" said Dennis. "You don't know the powers of the Menace! I'm not staying on a soppy nursery slope!"

He strapped himself onto his snowboard, pointed it down the mountain and set off after Cedric. After all his skateboarding through the streets of Beanotown, snowboarding was easy!

"Woohoo!" whooped Dennis as he powered down the slope, slicing through the white powdery snow. **"Awesome!"**

At the bottom of the slope he skidded to a halt and grinned. This holiday was gonna be a blast!

Dennis took the ski lift back up to the top of the mountain and whizzed down again, even faster this time. He practised a few jumps and swivels then jumped on the lift again.

Meanwhile, on the nursery slope, Dad had just fallen on his bottom for the nineteenth time. Mum was headfirst in a snowdrift.

"I think we're ready for our first proper ski!" bubbled the cheerful ski instructor. He and Dad pulled Mum out of the snowdrift and the beginners' class set off. They got on the same lift as Dennis and arrived at the top of the mountain at the same time.

The beginners started to wind their way slowly down the slope and Dennis chortled as he watched Dad trying to keep his balance. Then he spotted Cedric halfway down.

"I'll show that softy how menaces get down a mountain!" chuckled Dennis. He pushed off and sped down the mountain, but the beginners' class was taking up the whole slope!

"GANGWAY!"

bellowed Dennis as he plunged through the class, scattering new skiers right and left. Dad lost control of his skis and swerved off towards a large tree. Mum landed in another snowdrift. Bea did a jump on her baby snowboard and spun in the air as Dennis whizzed below her. Dennis was pleased with his little sister – she found snowboarding as easy as he did!

"You rascal!" hollered the ski instructor as he rounded up his scattered class. But Dennis was past! As he caught Cedric up, he pulled his catapult from his pocket and aimed a snowball at Cedric's backside. POW!

"YOWEE!"

Cedric clutched his bottom, dropped his ski poles and overbalanced, landing on his back in a snowy ditch and staring up at Dennis's grinning face.

"Did you lose your balance?" Dennis chuckled. "I can see you don't know everything about skiing after all!"

Dennis boarded on down the next slope and saw a group of softies wearing padded ski suits in pretty pastel colours, learning how to stop if they were going too fast.

"Huh, they need to learn how to go fast!" chuckled Dennis. "I'll give them a hand!" He sliced through the snow, weaving towards the softies. One of them turned and saw him.

"EEEEEEEEEK!" he shouted. "Ski away! Ski away!"

The whole group sped away from Dennis, whimpering, but they weren't fast enough!

"Make way!" roared Dennis as he crashed into seven softies at the same time. They clung to each other's waists to stop from falling and snaked down the slope in a trembling line, getting faster and faster. As Dennis curved around them, the softy in front panicked, changed direction and led all the others off the slope and into a heap in the snow.

At the bottom of the mountain, back on the nursery slope, Dennis unstrapped himself from his board and saw Bea speeding towards him. She stopped next to him and they watched as Dad arrived at the bottom of the mountain.

"Snowman!" Bea giggled as she pointed at Dad, who had pulled himself out of the snow but was still white all over.

"You've given me an idea, Bea!" chortled Dennis. "With all this snow, we should have some fun!"

Dennis and Bea made snow-monsters.

Lots of snow-monsters!

Huge, scary snow-monsters!

Ten minutes later, as the beginners and the softies snaked slowly down the nursery slope, they were horrified to see their path blocked by ten enormous white monsters!

"Yikes! It's the Yeti!" screamed the first softy.

"I can't stop!" yelled Mum.

"What a mega menace!" grinned Dennis as the softies and the beginners crashed into the huge snow-monsters he and Bea had built. Snow heads rolled in all directions. People were sticking halfway through the snow bodies. It was chaos! The ski instructor spotted Dennis and shook his fist.

Dennis used the ski lift to the very top of the steepest slope. He stood at the top and looked out over the mountain range. The sky was blue. The sun beat down. Dennis let out a whoop of menacing delight. The only thing that was missing was someone to race against! Then Dennis had one of his brilliant ideas. He quickly made a large snowball and positioned it on the edge of the slope. He would race the snowball to the bottom!

Dennis pointed his board down the mountain and pushed off, flicking the snowball at the same time. He scooted away, just ahead of the tumbling snowball! But as they got further down the slope, the snowball collected more and more snow. It got bigger and bigger! Dennis went even faster, with the enormous snowball close behind him. Just in time he reached the bottom and darted out of the way.

The beginners and the softies had just escaped from the snow-monsters when...

WHUMP!

The massive snowball hit them and tumbled them down again. Dennis roared with laughter.

But Dad had seen everything. He marched towards Dennis with the ski instructor. They were both covered in snow and looked furious. Dennis gave them a cheerful wave and jumped onto the ski lift just in time. He was carried away before they could reach him!

Then Dennis saw the ski instructor talking to the ski lift operator. Just as the ski lift was above deep snow, it stopped. Dennis dangled above, his fists clenched in fury.

"Let me down!" he bellowed. The ski instructor folded his arms and laughed.

"You'll stay up there until you've learned your lesson!" he shouted.

"And until we've had a nice, unmenaced ski!" added Dad.

Dennis watched in a rage as the beginners got onto the drag lifts and were carried back up to the top of the easiest slope. Then he looked down and a grin spread slowly across his face. Snowboarding was just like skateboarding – and he had done bigger jumps than this on a skateboard!

"Bombs away!" bellowed Dennis as he slipped out of the lift and dropped skilfully through the air to land on the soft snow. He sped down to catch the beginners, who were still on the drag lifts.

Dennis boarded past them, but his board was tipped at such an angle that he sprayed snow into their faces.

"Argghh!" yelled one.

"I can't see!" cried another.

One by one they lost their grip on the ski lift and fell like dominoes into the heavy snow.

As they rose up they looked like abominable snowmen!

"You... you..." spluttered the ski instructor, as Dennis whizzed past him.

"See you back at the chalet!" bellowed Dennis to Mum and Dad as they pulled themselves out of the snow. He whizzed to the foot of the mountain, unstrapped the board and tramped back to the chalet. No one was there.

Cedric was still stuck in a snowdrift. Everyone else was struggling to escape from the trail of chaos Dennis had left behind him.

Dennis grabbed a fistful of comics and a huge mug of hot chocolate, and settled down in the armchair beside the roaring fire.

"Now this is my idea of a relaxing holiday!" he chortled as he opened the first comic!

93

Written by RACHEL ELLIOT

Illustrated by BARRIE APPLEBY

published under licence by

meadowside
CHILDREN'S BOOKS

185 Fleet Street, London, EC4A 2HS